D0064935

The
Missing
Fossil Mystery

Emily Herman

Illustrated by Andrew Glass

Hyperion Books for Children
New York

Text © 1996 by Emily Herman.

Illustrations © 1996 by Andrew Glass.

Printed in the United States of America.

First Edition

1 3 5 7 9 10 8 6 4 2

The artwork for each picture is prepared using pencil.

This book is set in 16-point Berkeley Book.

Library of Congress Cataloging-in-Publication Data

Herman, Emily.
The missing fossil mystery / Emily Herman; illustrated by Andrew Glass—1st ed.
p.   cm. — (Hyperion chapters)
Summary: When Liza's older brother, Jesse, refuses to let her take his fossil to school for second grade show and share, she takes the trilobite anyway and loses it in the classroom.
ISBN 0-7868-0145-X (trade) — ISBN 0-7868-1091-2 (pbk.)
[1. Fossils—Fiction. 2. Schools—Fiction. 3. Brothers and sisters—Fiction.] I. Title. II. Series.
PZ7.H43135Mi   1996
[Fic]—dc20   95-21048

Table of Contents

To Dave, Ben, and Joanna, and to my
friends at Woolrich Central School
—E. M. H.

1
A Rock or a Fossil?

Liza wanted to take her brother Jesse's fossil to school, but Jesse wouldn't let her.

"Are you kidding?" he said. "My fossil is millions of years old. You might lose it or something."

"I would not. I'd take good care of it." Liza could imagine it in her hand, flat and almost smooth, except for some small, even ridges. The fossil reminded her of a sow bug—the lumpy grayish insectlike creature that scuttled away when she turned rocks over in the woods. But the fossil was black and still. It felt better than a sow bug. It felt like a stone with a secret. The secret was that it had been alive and lived in an ocean a long, long time ago.

"Please, Jesse?" Liza asked.

"No way," Jesse said. He zipped up his backpack and flung it over his shoulder. "It's my first trilobite fossil. When I'm a paleontologist I want to be able to look back and still have my first trilobite."

"When you're a what?"

"A paleontologist. A person who studies fossils."

"I'm going to be a pal . . . pale . . ."

"Yeah, right. Listen. Take a rock to school. Tell them it's a fossil. Second graders wouldn't know the difference."

Liza stomped up the stairs. That dumb Jesse. Second graders would too know what's a rock and what's a fossil.

What else could she take for show and share?

Maybe she could take something of her

3

sister's. Sarah had already left for school, but Liza could sneak into her room and . . .

No. Ever since the diary incident, Sarah had made it clear that Liza was forbidden to touch anything in her room.

Liza went into her own room. She looked at the treasures on her collection shelf. What *could* she take for show and share? The old ink bottle? No. She had already taken it to school. The owl pellet? No. She had already taken that to school, too. Besides, when the kids heard what it was—owl spit-up—they were so noisy that she couldn't point out the neat mouse bones and bird feathers embedded in the lump. She looked at her rocks. She picked up a small, bumpy one. Could she take it to school? It was almost the same size as Jesse's fossil. It was almost the same

4

color. *Could* she call it a fossil? No. Second graders would be able to tell the difference between a rock and a fossil.

Then Liza got an idea that made her face hot just thinking about it. Second graders would know, but a certain fifth grader might not. What if she replaced the fossil on Jesse's collection shelf with her rock that looked almost the same? Jesse would never know. When she got home from school, she could change it back. Then she could say, "*Fifth graders don't know the difference between a rock and a fossil.*" She would say it only to herself, but it still would make her laugh.

Quickly, while Jesse was eating breakfast downstairs, she made the switch.

2
The Big Switch

Liza kept the fossil in her mitten all the way to school. Sometimes she held it in her hand. Sometimes she let it rattle against her fingers. It felt like a smile, hidden away in the tip of her mitten. And every time she glanced at Jesse she thought, Fifth graders wouldn't even know.

She kept it secret until show and share time. Good thing show and share came almost first thing.

"This is a fossil," Liza said when it was her turn. "It is very, very old. Millions of years. It looks like a sow bug a little, but it

isn't. It is called a trilobite. Any questions or comments?"

She knew the questions or comments she would get. Gracie would say, "That's neat. What kind of animal was it really?" Kyle would say he had one, too. Kristen would want to hold it. And Stephanie would want to know where Liza bought it. Stephanie always wanted to know where people bought things. Even things you could get anywhere, like notebooks with swirly designs on the front. Even things you found outside, like snail shells. So she was ready when Stephanie asked.

"Oh, it's been in the family," Liza said. "My uncle sent it to us."

Ms. Bauer raised her hand. "Did he dig it up? Is he a paleontologist?"

9

Paleontologist. Liza liked that word. "No," she said, "but I am going to be one."

"What's a paleontologist?" asked Alex.

"Someone who finds fossils and studies them," Liza said.

"And who uses fossils to understand what life was like millions of years ago and how it has changed," Ms. Bauer added.

"Like dinosaurs," said Alex.

"Yes," said Ms. Bauer. "But trilobites are even older—five hundred million years old!"

Then show and share was over. It was time for snack. Liza kept her fossil on the corner of her desk so she could watch it. Every time she looked at it she smiled. She smiled because it had been a great show and share. She smiled because she was tricking Jesse. And she smiled because it was amazing to have something on her desk that was so old that she couldn't even write how old it was. She didn't know how many zeros the number five hundred million had.

3
Newspaper Day

After snacktime was over, Ms. Bauer announced it was Newspaper Day. They would cover all their usual subjects but would use newspapers to study them. First they had a newspaper scavenger hunt, to get used to finding things in the paper. Everyone had their own newspaper. They had to circle a sports article in blue and an advertisement in red. They had to underline the day's date and put a box around the name of their town. They had to find the TV listings and the weather map and the table of contents. Then they each had to find one article that they wanted to share with the class.

"I found an article about a moose," Gracie said. "I'll share that."

"I want to share more about fossils," Liza said. "Did you see an article about them?"

"No," Gracie said. "Hey, the date is on every page." She already had crossed four things off her scavenger list.

Liza underlined the date. Then she looked for other things on her list. The newspaper was awkward to read. The inside pages fell out and then the advertisements slid off her desk. Other kids had trouble with the newspaper, too. Kyle had crumpled some of his pages and was throwing them away. As he passed Liza's desk, he picked up the trilobite.

"It really does feel like a rock," he said. "Are you sure it isn't?"

"Hey," Liza said. "Put that down."

Kyle tossed it up and caught it. "Is it worth a lot?"

"Kyle," Liza said.

"Ignore him," Gracie said. "Then he'll go away."

"Three minutes for finishing up," Ms. Bauer called. "We'll share our articles after art."

Liza hadn't read an article.

She hadn't found half the things on her list.

And Kyle still had Jesse's fossil. He put his hand in his pocket. "Thanks for giving it to me," he said, and started to walk away.

Liza jumped up. The newspapers fell off her desk. "It's not . . ." She wondered what she could say. "It's not yours to touch," she said.

"Want me to get Ms. Bauer?" Gracie asked.

"Just kidding. Just kidding," Kyle said.

15

He put the fossil back on the corner of Liza's desk. Liza quickly put it in her pocket. It would be safe there for the rest of the day.

4
Chocolate, Plain, or Skim?

Once a week they had to swish with fluoride rinse for strong teeth, so after art, that's what they did. Disgusting! Especially the part about spitting the rinse back into the pouch.

During math they had to find all the numbers from one to one hundred in the newspaper. Scraps of paper littered the class-room like snow.

After lunch Ms. Bauer said, "Since today

is Newspaper Day, I would like you to write an article for our class paper."

"Does it have to be real?" Kyle asked.

"Yes," said Ms. Bauer.

"What about comics? Can we do comics?" Alex asked.

Liza didn't listen to the answer. She knew what she was going to write about. She took the trilobite out of her pocket and put it on the corner of her desk to describe it.

"Trilobites look like bugs, but they aren't," she wrote. "They are fossils. They lived . . ." She wasn't sure what to write next. She looked through the real newspaper to see what kinds of things writers put in articles. The articles had a lot of information. Maybe there was a book about fossils on the Discovery Shelf. She went to look.

There were a lot of books about dinosaurs. There were lots of books about stars and insects and birds and sea creatures like sharks and whales.

"I think trilobites are more like lobsters or spiders, but you'll need to find a book about ancient animals," Ms. Bauer said when Liza asked her. "Let's see what we can find." She reached for a book on the shelf.

Just then there was a knock on the door. "Ms. Bauer, we're doing a survey for math. Is this a good time to ask your class some questions?" It was Jesse's voice.

Liza looked up. She always liked it when Jesse visited her class. She was glad she was sitting right next to Ms. Bauer. That way Jesse would be sure to notice her.

Suddenly, Liza remembered the fossil. It

was in plain sight on her desk, right next to her newspaper! Say no, Ms. Bauer, Liza thought. Say no.

But Ms. Bauer said, "I think we can take a little break."

Jesse and his friend Michael came in. Michael said, "OK. Actually this is part of a school improvement plan for the cafeteria. We fifth graders think things could be better there. Our first question is: Would you rather drink chocolate milk, plain milk, low-fat, or skim?"

"Raise your hands and we'll count," Jesse added.

Liza kept her head down. What should she do? Should she go over to her desk and cover the fossil? Should she take the hall tag and pretend to need a drink? She didn't even

know if she should look up at Jesse. She usually looked up for surveys. She always grinned at Jesse when he visited her class room, even when he ignored her. But her face was red. She could feel it, hot and prickly. One look at her and Jesse would know. Maybe he knew anyway and that was why he'd come in.

Liza glanced at her desk. The fossil was obvious from where Liza was sitting. But maybe from where Jesse was standing, the newspaper covered the fossil or at least hid it in shadows. No. Liza was almost positive that Jesse could see the fossil if he looked. But maybe he'd think it was a rock. After all, he didn't think second graders could tell the difference between a rock and a fossil. Could *he* tell? Liza was sure he could if he looked closely enough.

But he was looking at the clipboard. Michael counted hands and Jesse wrote down numbers. Liza raised her hand when Michael said "skim."

"Next question," Michael said. "If you could get salad stuff from a salad bar, would you eat it?"

"Would it just be rabbit food or would there be good stuff, too?" Kyle asked.

Michael and Jesse walked a little closer to Kyle's desk. That meant they were closer to Liza's desk, too.

"What's good stuff?" Jesse asked.

"Things like croutons and bacon and pickles."

"Maybe sometimes," Michael answered, "but mostly rabbit food."

"Any more questions?" Jesse asked. Liza watched as he searched around the classroom, looking for raised hands. She wondered if she should raise hers as a distraction. But she couldn't think of anything to say.

Finally Michael said, "OK, so who would get salad?" Liza watched as he and Jesse counted hands. At last Jesse's head bent back down over the clipboard as he wrote down the information.

"Can we make suggestions for the salad bar?" Gracie asked.

Liza waited as people suggested everything from pickled mushrooms to chocolate chips. She waited and waited and waited until Jesse and Michael were gone. Then she took the hall tag and went to get a drink of water, just to cool off.

When Liza got back, everyone was cleaning up for afternoon recess.

"No one's going out until this room is picked up," Ms. Bauer said. Everyone was taking her words seriously. They were folding newspapers. They were crumpling cut or torn pages and wadding up advertisements to throw away. The wastebasket was overflowing, but Kyle had one foot in it and was stomping it down. Gracie and Alex were crawling under desks on their hands and knees, picking up every last scrap.

"Do you want to play dinosaurs grazing for paper?" Gracie asked as Liza passed her.

"Sure," Liza said. "Just one thing." She went to her desk. There was her writing. There was the newspaper, neatly folded. But when she picked up the newspaper and reached for the trilobite, it wasn't on the corner of her desk. It wasn't on the floor under her desk. It wasn't anywhere at all.

5
Gone!

"I can't find my trilobite!" Liza cried.

"Somebody took it probably," Kyle said.

Liza and Gracie looked at him. "Not me!" he added.

"Before we blame anyone, let's look around," Ms. Bauer said.

Even though everyone shook newspapers and looked under desks and around the room, the fossil was gone.

28

"Don't worry, Liza. I'm sure it will turn up," Ms. Bauer said.

All the other kids in her class were pulling on their coats and boots and mittens. They were lining up at the door for afternoon recess. Liza stood by her coat hook.

She wished she could look in Kyle's backpack. She wished she could look in everyone's desk. She wished the room was quiet so that she could think about where the fossil might be. She wished she had put it in her backpack right after show and share. She wished she hadn't taken it at all. This was going to be even worse than Sarah's diary.

"Out, Liza," Ms. Bauer commanded as everyone else jostled out of the room. "I have to make a phone call and you can't stay in the room alone."

"It wasn't my fossil," Liza whispered to Gracie on the playground. "It was Jesse's."

Gracie's eyes widened. "And he doesn't know you have it?"

Liza shook her head. "He said I *couldn't* have it. He said I'd lose it."

"Uh-oh." Gracie thought for a minute. "Do you think Kyle took it?"

"I don't know," Liza said. "Maybe even Jesse took it, to teach me a lesson." Liza looked around the playground. One duty teacher was talking to Stephanie and a first grader. The other was shooting baskets with a bunch of third graders. "I've got to find it.

I've got to go back in."

"Ms. Bauer will kill you if she finds out," Gracie whispered.

"But I've got to get the fossil back to Jesse."

6

Time Is Running Out

Liza waited until no one was looking. She went inside the school. She walked down the hall. When Mr. Woodward walked toward her, she ducked into the bathroom. When Mrs. Boomer walked toward her, she took a drink. All the time she was walking, her mind was working. She was thinking about plans and she was thinking about excuses. Finally she decided she should go

33

to Jesse's classroom first. If she saw him, maybe she could tell right away whether he took the fossil or not. Maybe she would confess and get it over with.

Usually Gracie went with her when she went into the third, fourth, and fifth grade wing of the school. Liza knew where Jesse's classroom was, but she didn't know the teachers in that wing very well and she wasn't very comfortable with some of the older kids. Sure enough, there were a couple of fifth graders hanging outside the door to the boys' room. Fortunately they were so busy with each other, they didn't notice her.

She looked in a third grade classroom. Everyone was sitting at desks, writing.

She looked in a fourth grade classroom. Everyone was sitting at desks, listening to the teacher.

Finally she came to Jesse's classroom. She looked in the room. Kids were in small clusters, talking, arguing, writing, drawing. No Jesse.

"Hey, Mrs. K.," one girl said, and pointed at the door.

Jesse's teacher looked up at Liza. "May I help you?" she asked.

"I'm looking for my brother, Jesse," Liza whispered.

Mrs. Kawaguchi looked around the classroom. So did Liza. Jesse wasn't there. Michael was missing, too.

"He's in my group," another girl said. Liza recognized her. Melanie. "They're still doing surveys."

"Do you need something?" Mrs. Kawaguchi asked.

Liza shook her head. "That's OK," she said, but she was thinking that she didn't have much time left to find the fossil.

7
Wastebasket Dig

When Liza got to her classroom, she stood still.

If Jesse has it, there is nothing I can do, she thought. If Kyle has it, it might be in his desk. But Liza knew she would really get in trouble if she got caught looking through Kyle's desk. Instead she looked around the room.

Newspapers covered desks, but Liza and

her classmates had already checked the tops of desks. The floor was mostly picked up. Crumpled newspapers filled the wastebasket.

The wastebasket! Liza decided to dig through that.

Liza dragged the overflowing wastebasket over to the Discovery Table. Someone had emptied the pencil sharpener on the very top, just before recess. There were some crumpled-up rough drafts of articles, too. She put them in a pile on the table.

The next layer she found was of cut-up advertising fliers. That was from math, when they had to find all the numbers from one to one hundred.

Then there was a layer of envelopes full of fluoride rinse. Wrinkling her nose and holding her breath, she lifted one out.

"What are you doing, Liza?" Ms. Bauer asked from the doorway.

"Oh!" Liza let out a gasp.

Ms. Bauer took a step closer. "I thought I'd sent you out."

Liza talked fast. "But I have to find the fossil. It was Jesse's fossil. He told me not to take it." Liza shook her head. "He said take a rock. He said second graders couldn't tell the difference."

"Oh," Ms. Bauer said. "Oh," she said again as she went over the day in her head. She went to her desk. She pulled out a pair of rubber gloves. "You should use these," was all she said.

Liza went back to work. When she had moved the last fluoride rinse envelope she

breathed again. Then she said, "Look. Last we had writing. Before that we had math. Before that, we rinsed. And this proves we had art." She held up Kyle's picture. They were supposed to have drawn a picture from a fairy tale, but Kyle drew an alien in a spaceship. Kyle always drew aliens. He always threw his pictures away, too. He never took them home.

"Do you know what you are?" Ms. Bauer said.

In trouble? Liza wondered. She shook her head.

"You're a paleontologist."

"I am?"

"Sure. You are going through layers, one at a time, hunting for a fossil, and at the same time, you are finding out what happened in school today."

"I know what happened," Liza said, "but I haven't found the fossil yet, and I'm at snacktime."

"Fossils sometimes shift," Ms. Bauer said. "If there's an earthquake or something."

42

Liza remembered Kyle stomping on the papers in the wastebasket. "Kyle is like an earthquake, isn't he?"

Ms. Bauer smiled. "That's a good description of Kyle," she said.

The wastebasket was almost empty. Liza could see banana peels and empty chip bags. All that was left was one crumpled up newspaper. Liza lifted it a little way out . . .

. . . and heard a tiny clunk.

Something small and hard. It might be a rock. It might be a peach pit. It might be Jesse's fossil. She tilted the wastebasket and reached in.

There, at the very bottom, right next to a pear core, was something small and dark. Liza curled her fingers around the lump and tucked it in her palm. She couldn't feel it very well

through the rubber gloves, but she was
pretty sure . . .

"Hi, Ms. Bauer." It was Jesse! "Mrs. K.
said Liza came looking for me."

Ms. Bauer looked over the top of her
glasses at Jesse, then glanced at Liza, kneel-
ing next to the wastebasket. She didn't say
anything.

Then Jesse noticed Liza. "Oh, there you

are, Liza. What happened? Mrs. K. said you looked worried. Got in trouble? What did you need me for?"

"Nothing," Liza said. "Nothing at all."

Jesse shrugged. "OK. See you around."

Once he'd left the room, Liza opened her fingers, to see what she was holding. It was the trilobite fossil. She looked up at Ms. Bauer. "I've got it," she whispered.

"Good job," Ms. Bauer said. Then, in a news broadcaster's voice she said, "Today a young paleontologist discovered a trilobite fossil in a wastebasket dig. Then, after cleaning up the Discovery Table . . . ," Ms. Bauer looked at her sternly over the tops of her glasses, ". . . she returned the fossil to its rightful owner."

"I will. I will. It's been such a desperate

day," Liza said. She held the fossil in a tight fist. How could she keep it absolutely safe until the end of the day? She thought for a minute, then put it in the toe of her shoe. "I'll feel it every step," she said.

"A good reminder," Ms. Bauer said. "Now, clean up."

"Ms. Bauer," Liza said as she threw everything away again, "will you help me spell *paleontologist*?"

PALEONTOLOGIST

8
Shoelaces and Secrets

Of all days for Jesse to come straight home, Liza thought as she rode home on the bus, three seats behind him. He always went to Michael's house or played basketball or stayed after school for something. At least I can put the fossil back when he stops for a peanut butter sandwich or a glass of milk, she thought.

She really wanted to wash the fossil,

though. She'd rinsed it off in the girls' room, holding it carefully so that it wouldn't go down the drain. But after digging through the wastebasket and smelling the rotten banana peels smeared with yogurt, she couldn't get the trilobite clean enough. There was also a little brownish lump on it that she couldn't remove with her fingernail. Was it chocolate? Had it always been there? She needed time.

Jesse didn't give her any. He ran up the front walk, through the door, and halfway up the stairs before Liza could think of a way to stop him.

"Jesse," she called, without the slightest idea of what to say next.

"What?" He didn't even slow down.

"I've got a knot in my lace."

"I gotta get my basketball cards. Michael and I are having a super trade."

Liza slumped down. Jesse kept his basketball cards on the shelf right above his trilobite. He was going to run up to his room, find the missing fossil, come down, and . . .

She heard the thump of his backpack on the floor. She heard a whoop. She heard his bedroom door slam. She heard his clumping footsteps down the stairs. She didn't look up, even though she knew he was standing over her.

"Which shoe?" he asked.

"Huh?"

"Which lace has a knot?" he asked. "I don't have all day."

Without thinking, Liza stuck out her right shoe, the one with the trilobite in it. Jesse squatted down and grunted a little as he struggled with the knot. "You sure didn't want this to come undone, did you?" he said, but at last he got it. "There. I'm out of here. Tell Mom."

"OK. Thanks, Jesse," she yelled after him. As soon as he was out the door, she ran upstairs and scrubbed the fossil. She even used toothpaste and her own toothbrush. Then she dried it carefully and set it on his shelf, beside his gyroscope.

His gyroscope. Hmmm. If she could learn to make that work, it would be a great show and share for next week. Liza reached out to touch it, stopped, and instead picked up the stone she'd left in

place of the fossil. I'd better put this in my shoe, she thought, to help me remember.

9
Second Grade Times

SECOND GRADE TIMES

Paleontologist Uncovers Trilobite!
Discovers History of Second Grade Day

Liza McNear discovered a missing fossil in the wastebasket of her classroom on Tuesday, March 9. She also found out what happened during that day. Lots of times, a paleontologist goes backward. Last we had writing. Before that we had math. Before that we rinsed with fluoride. (Yuck!) Before that we had art. Before that we had a newspaper scavenger hunt. Before that we had snack.

Sometimes fossils get shifted around because of earthquakes.

A paleontologist is a little like a detective. It is a messy job. It is good to wear gloves.

"What a great article," Liza's mother said when she read it aloud at the supper table.

"The lead story," Liza's father said. "Good job!"

"Great headlines," Sarah said.

"Ms. Bauer wrote the headlines, but I helped," Liza said. "And I wrote the article exactly by myself." She was watching Jesse. Jesse was watching her.

"Just a minute," Jesse said. He left the table and ran up the stairs, two steps at a time. He came back down more slowly and sat in his chair. "About this fossil . . . ," Jesse said.

Liza looked at him and shook her head. "Some people just can't tell the difference," she said.